P9-AOW-682

Princess PULVERIZER

worse, worser, wurst

PENGUIN WORKSHOP
Penguin Young Readers Group
An Imprint of Penguin Random House LLC

Text copyright © 2018 by Nancy Krulik. Illustrations copyright © 2018
by Ben Balistreri. All rights reserved. Published by Penguin Workshop,
an imprint of Penguin Random House LLC, 345 Hudson Street,
New York, New York 10014. PENGUIN and PENGUIN WORKSHOP
are trademarks of Penguin Books, Ltd, and the W colophon is a trademark
of Penguin Random House LLC. Printed in the USA.

Library of Congress Cataloging-in-Publication Data is available.

ISBN 9780515158342 (pbk)   10 9 8 7 6 5 4 3 2 1
ISBN 9780515158359 (hc)   10 9 8 7 6 5 4 3 2 1

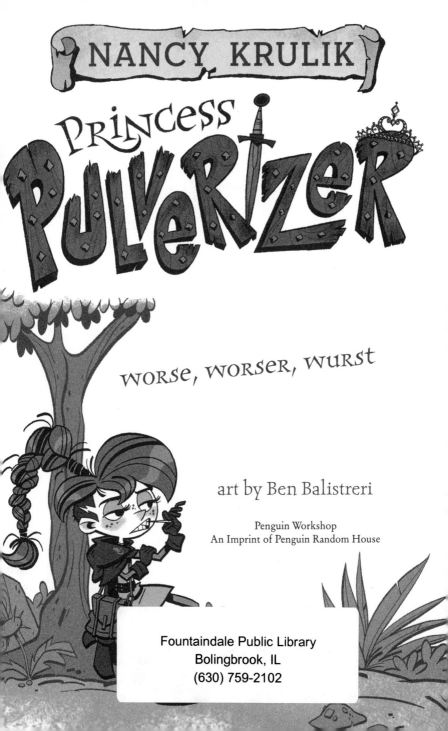

NANCY KRULIK

PRINCESS PULVERIZER

worse, worser, wurst

art by Ben Balistreri

Penguin Workshop
An Imprint of Penguin Random House

For my grandparents Sadie and Max, who were always really good at making me laugh—NK

To the memory of my second golden retriever, Beaker, the jolliest dog I've ever known and a pooch who would have loved a good liverwurst sandwich—BB

CHAPTER 1

"AAAAAHHH! There's a MONSTER in that tree!" Lucas cried out. "A hairy, creepy-crawly MONSTER!"

The scared knight-in-training dropped the grilled cheese sandwich he'd been snacking on and ran off as fast as he could.

"A *monster*?" Princess Pulverizer repeated. But she did not sound scared at all.

Nothing scared Princess Pulverizer.

Well, *very little* scared her, anyway.

"Y-y-yes," Lucas answered from his favorite hiding spot—crouched behind his best friend, Dribble the dragon. "I hate things that creep and crawl!"

"I'll defeat it!" Princess Pulverizer said, leaping to her feet.

"H-h-how?" Lucas stammered nervously. "You don't have any weapons."

"Sure I do." The princess bent her arms to show off her muscles. "These!"

Lucas and Dribble did not seem particularly impressed.

But that wasn't stopping Princess Pulverizer. "*Watch out, monster! You are no match for me,*" she shouted.

Princess Pulverizer looked up into the tree. But she didn't see a monster. She didn't see anything other than the usual branches, leaves, and blossoms.

Hmmm . . . Maybe the monster was hiding.

The princess leaped into the air and grabbed a tree branch. She pulled herself up and began climbing, searching for a monster hidden in the leaves.

But there was no monster anywhere.

Suddenly, out of the corner of her eye, Princess Pulverizer noticed a black, white, and yellow hairy creature creeping and crawling on a branch.

Wait a minute.

Hairy?

Creeping?

Crawling?

Oh brother. Lucas hadn't seen a monster at all. He'd seen a *caterpillar.*

Princess Pulverizer wasn't surprised that

Lucas was afraid of an insect. Lucas was afraid of *everything*.

The princess let the little caterpillar crawl onto her finger. She tucked him in her pocket and slid down to the ground.

Princess Pulverizer walked over to her friends and dangled the tiny creature in front of Lucas's nose. "Is this your monster?"

Lucas shuddered. "Get that away from me!" he cried out.

Princess Pulverizer laughed.

Dribble looked from the caterpillar to Lucas and back again. He clenched his dragon lips together tightly, trying not to laugh. But he couldn't help himself.

"Ha-ha-ha-ha . . ." *SNORT!* Dribble laughed so hard, the ground shook beneath him.

"This isn't a monster," Princess Pulverizer told Lucas. "It's a caterpillar." She placed the stunned insect back on a low-hanging tree branch.

Lucas turned red with embarrassment. "I really hate things that creep and crawl," he said timidly.

"Aaaachoooo!" Suddenly, Dribble let out a loud, powerful sneeze.

"Gesundheit," Lucas said. "Are you getting a cold?"

The dragon shook his head. "It's those apple blossoms. I'm allergic. Aaachoooo!"

That last sneeze was so strong, it blew Lucas over. He fell backward onto the ground.

"Sorry," Dribble apologized as Lucas scrambled back to his feet.

"It's okay," Lucas assured him.

The dragon looked down at the grilled cheese sandwich his friend had dropped. "What a waste of cheese," he said. "It's too bad you didn't finish it. Gouda grilled

cheese is my specialty."

"I'm sorry," Lucas apologized. "But it's not a total waste. The ants seem to be enjoying it."

"I'm sorry, too," Princess Pulverizer grumbled. "I'm sorry I couldn't save you from a creepy-crawly, hairy monster. Because that would have been a good deed."

"A very good deed *in*deed," Lucas agreed.

"But saving you from a caterpillar is not

the same thing," Princess Pulverizer said sadly. "Now I *still* need to do seven more good deeds before I can go to Knight School."

Lucas and Dribble knew what Princess Pulverizer meant. Before they had met her, she had spent her days with Lady Frump at the Royal School of Ladylike Manners, where she was taught to pour tea properly and dance the saltarello at royal balls. Things all princesses needed to know.

Only Princess Pulverizer didn't want to be a princess.

She wanted to be a knight.

So she had begged her father, King Alexander of Empiria, to let her go to Knight School. Unfortunately, the king told her she *couldn't* go—at least not until she went on a Quest of Kindness and performed eight good deeds.

So far, the princess had only completed one good deed—retrieving the Queen of Shmergermeister's jewels from the evil ogre who had stolen them.

That left seven more deeds to go. Which Princess Pulverizer was sure she could accomplish—especially since she now had Lucas and Dribble to help her.

To an outsider, Dribble and Lucas probably didn't seem like they would be very helpful. After all, Lucas was such a fraidy-cat, the other boys had nicknamed him Lucas the Lily-Livered and laughed him out of Knight School. And Dribble had been thrown out of his lair because the other dragons didn't like that he used his fire for making grilled cheese sandwiches rather than burning villages.

But Lucas and Dribble were loyal.

And nice.

And really willing to help.

They were just the kind of pals a girl trying to get into Knight School needed to have around.

"This place is boring," Princess Pulverizer told her friends. She pulled a toothpick from her knapsack and used the thin sliver of wood to pick rye bread seeds out from between her teeth.

"I don't think Lady Frump would have liked to see you doing that," Dribble teased her.

Princess Pulverizer laughed. "Lady Frump didn't like anything I did. I was her worst student ever."

"But you'll do great in Knight School," Lucas assured her.

"I won't get to *go* to Knight School if we don't find someone who needs my help," Princess Pulverizer told him. "I'm ready for a new adventure."

"That makes one of us," Lucas muttered under his breath.

"Aaaachooo!" Dribble sneezed again.

The dragon's powerful sneeze blew the caterpillar right out of the tree and onto the ground. That poor guy was not having a good day at all.

"Come on!" Princess Pulverizer said as she started walking out of the forest.

Despite the fact that they weren't looking for adventure, Dribble and Lucas followed close behind her.

Just as the princess knew they would.

After all, nobody argued with Princess Pulverizer.

Well, *almost* nobody, anyway.

CHAPTER 2

"Mmmm . . ." Princess Pulverizer sniffed at the air excitedly. She and her friends had wandered into a nearby kingdom. Something smelled delicious. "What is that?"

"I think it's salami," Lucas replied. "It's coming from the food stands over there."

"This could be the perfect place for me to sell my sandwiches," Dribble thought out loud. "Who doesn't love a grilled salami and cheese on rye?"

The dragon's mouth watered at the thought of such a delicious treat—which left a big puddle of dragon drool below him.

"Aaaahhh!" Just then, a passing villager spotted the big, green, drooling dragon. He screamed and ran away as fast as he could.

Princess Pulverizer frowned. "It *would* be the perfect spot—if you could somehow get people to stop running away from you long enough to try your food," she told the dragon.

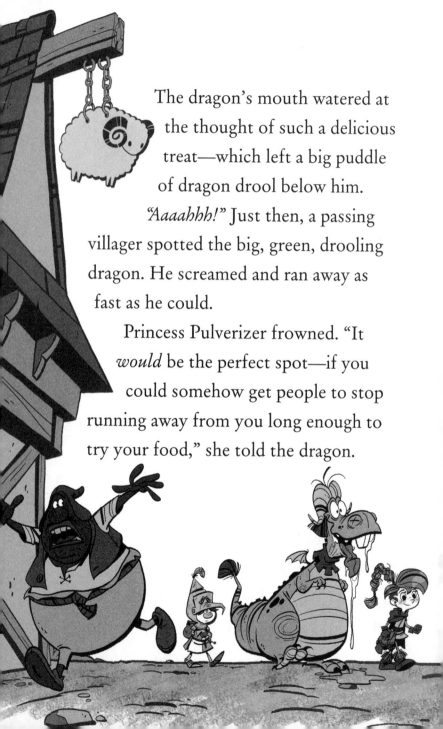

Dribble shook his head. "I just don't get why people are so afraid of me." He flashed his friendliest smile at Princess Pulverizer. "Do I look scary to you?"

The princess stared at the dragon's huge teeth.

She looked down at his long, sharp claws.

She glanced up at his big, bulgy eyes.

Yeah, Dribble could look pretty scary, if you didn't know him.

But Princess Pulverizer was trying hard to be kind these days. So all she said was, "Um . . . no. You don't seem scary at all. At least not to me."

"Exactly," Dribble said. He smiled wider—which just made his eyes bulge more.

"YIKES!" a woman shouted as she caught sight of him. "I'M OUT OF HERE!"

"There goes another one," Dribble said sadly. His smile drooped. "I don't think I like this village anymore."

"Me either," Princess Pulverizer said.

"Why not?" Lucas asked her.

"Because there's no one here who needs saving," Princess Pulverizer told him. "Listen. Do you hear anyone asking for help?"

Lucas and Dribble listened. But they heard nothing.

Not a shriek.

Or a wail.

Or even a stressful sigh.

"See what I mean?" Princess Pulverizer asked them. "There are no adventures to be had here. We may as well leave."

"I agree," Lucas said. "I don't know what it is, but there's something creepy about this place."

"I'll tell you what it is," Dribble said. "Everyone here is miserable."

Princess Pulverizer looked around. Dribble was right. Not one person was smiling. There was no joy anywhere.

Not a giggle.

Or a guffaw.

Or even a tee-hee.

"Hmmm," Princess Pulverizer mused as she took another look around. "Maybe there *is* something going on here . . ."

"I don't like the sound of that," Lucas whispered nervously to Dribble.

Before Dribble could answer him, Princess Pulverizer stopped a pouting passerby in the square.

"Excuse me, sir." She introduced herself. "I'm Princess Pulverizer."

"Pleased to meet you," the man replied. "I'm Peter Pastrami."

"Nice to meet *you*," Princess Pulverizer

said. "I was just wondering if you could tell me why—"

"*Is that a dragon?*" Peter Pastrami interrupted her nervously. He pointed to Dribble.

"Oh, that's just Dribble," Princess Pulverizer replied. "He won't hurt you."

"*Just* Dribble?" the dragon repeated angrily. "Seriously?"

"He looks mad," Peter Pastrami insisted.

"He's harmless," the princess assured him. "Anyway, as I was saying, can you tell me why everyone here seems so sad?"

"Salamistonia wasn't always a cheerless place," Peter Pastrami replied, pulling at his beard. "Our kingdom was once very joyful, full of joking, laughter, and tickle fights."

"I love tickle fights," Lucas said. "No one gets hurt in a tickle fight."

Peter Pastrami nodded. "But that was before our beloved court jester, Lester, was kidnapped. With him gone, there's no one to make us laugh."

Princess Pulverizer's ears perked up at the word *kidnapped*. People who were kidnapped needed rescuing. And rescuing was a good deed!

"Do you know who kidnapped Lester?" the princess asked.

"The evil Wizard of Wurst," Peter Pastrami replied. "Lester was always pulling practical jokes on him."

"What kinds of jokes?" Princess Pulverizer inquired.

"Harmless stuff, really," Peter Pastrami answered. "Like putting mustard in his ketchup bottle or hiding his mayonnaise."

"I hate mayonnaise," Lucas said. "It's slimy."

"I know," Peter Pastrami agreed. "Why would anyone put it on a sandwich?"

"Well, actually," Dribble argued, "if you spread a little mayo on the bread before you grill—"

"Can we get back to the kidnapping?" Princess Pulverizer interrupted. "Do you know where the Wizard of Wurst is keeping Lester?"

Peter Pastrami nodded. "He's got him locked in his tower."

"Hasn't anyone tried to rescue him?" Princess Pulverizer pressed.

Peter nodded. "Sure. But no one has been able to do it. Even our kingdom's bravest knight, Sir Loin, came up short. He had to return to Salamistonia without Lester—which was embarrassing, since he had never failed at anything before."

"Why did he fail?" Princess Pulverizer asked.

Peter Pastrami shrugged. "He didn't have what it took to open the lock and free Lester."

"You mean the key?" Princess Pulverizer wondered aloud.

"It takes more than a key to open *that* lock," Peter Pastrami explained. "Rumor has it that the lock is magical. It will only open for someone who is selfless and pure of heart."

Princess Pulverizer thought for a moment. "What does *that* mean?" she asked.

Before Peter could answer, Dribble let out a loud belch. A tiny spark of dragon fire escaped from his mouth.

"Excuse me," Dribble said. "Sometimes gouda gives me heartburn."

But Peter Pastrami hadn't waited around to hear Dribble's explanation. At the first sight of dragon fire, he'd taken off down the road as fast as he could.

"If I were you, I'd get out of here," Peter called back to the princess. "The sadness of Salamistonia is very contagious."

"C-c-contagious?" Lucas stammered nervously. "I don't want to catch sadness. It's bad enough that I'm scared all the time. I don't want to be sad all the time, too."

"Me either," Dribble told Princess Pulverizer with a frown. "It wouldn't be fun cooking for people who don't smile when they eat. And I don't like the way

Peter Pastrami ran off without saying goodbye. That was rude."

Lucas gave Dribble a strange look. "Why are you doing that?" he asked him.

"Doing what?" Dribble wondered.

"Frowning," Lucas said. "You hardly ever frown. You're usually a happy dragon."

"I don't feel very happy right now," Dribble replied.

"Uh-oh," Lucas said.

"Uh-oh, what?" Princess Pulverizer asked him.

"I think Dribble is catching the Salamistonia sadness." Lucas frowned, too. "And that's making *me* feel sad. It *is* contagious. We should get out of this place."

"I agree," Princess Pulverizer said.

"We're leaving Salamistonia."

"We are?" Lucas sounded surprised.

"Sure," Princess Pulverizer replied. "We can't rescue Lester the Jester from the evil wizard if we stay here. Which means we're off to visit the Wizard of Wurst!"

Lucas shook his head. "That's not what I meant," he said with a sigh.

But it was too late. Princess Pulverizer had found someone to save. There was no stopping her now.

CHAPTER 3

"This is a bad idea," Lucas moaned as he trudged through the forest behind Princess Pulverizer and Dribble.

"Why?" Princess Pulverizer asked. "We were looking for a good deed to do, and now we have one."

"*You* were looking for a good deed to do," Lucas insisted. "I just wanted to get out of Salamistonia."

"Me, we, same thing," Princess Pulverizer said.

"Not exactly," Lucas said nervously.

"Are you sure we're going the right way?" Dribble asked Princess Pulverizer. "We've been walking a really long time."

"Oh, I'm sure. Read the signs." The princess pointed to the warnings posted on the nearby trees.

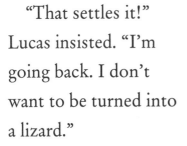

"That settles it!" Lucas insisted. "I'm going back. I don't want to be turned into a lizard."

"Don't worry," Princess Pulverizer told Lucas. "You and Dribble aren't going into the Wizard of Wurst's tower. Only I am."

Lucas stopped and looked at her. "I don't want *you* to be turned into a lizard, either."

"I won't be," Princess Pulverizer promised. Although she wasn't entirely sure it was the truth.

BEWARE OF WIZARD!

TRESPASSERS WILL BE TURNED INTO **LIZARDS!** TURN BACK BEFORE YOU MAKE THE **WURST MIS-STEAK** OF YOUR **LIFE!**

"How exactly do you plan to get into the wizard's tower?" Dribble asked. "You can't just walk in uninvited."

"I haven't figured that part out yet," Princess Pulverizer admitted. "I guess I'll have to trick him into inviting me in."

"Trick him?" Dribble asked. "You're going to trick a wizard?"

"Sure," Princess Pulverizer replied confidently. "It worked before. I fooled the ogre into letting me into his castle when I found out he'd stolen jewels from the Queen of Shmergermeister."

"Ogres aren't known for their brains," Lucas pointed out. "They're easy to fool. But wizards are smart."

"Judging by these signs, *this* wizard is also really mean," Dribble added.

"Wizards have magic," Lucas warned.

"They turn people into frogs, bats, and even mosquitoes—which is really bad, because bats *eat* mosquitoes. You don't want to get eaten, do you?"

Princess Pulverizer didn't answer Lucas's question.

She hadn't even *heard* Lucas's question.

In fact, she hadn't heard a single thing he'd said after the word *magic*.

"*Magic*," Princess Pulverizer repeated excitedly. "I'll use *magic* to get into that tower."

"Um . . . I hate to be the one to point this out, but you don't have magic powers," Dribble said. "You don't even know any magic spells. You're not a wizard."

Princess Pulverizer smiled broadly. "*Exactly*," she agreed mysteriously.

CHAPTER 4

"Okay, you two stay here and hide in the forest," Princess Pulverizer told Dribble and Lucas a while later, as they stopped near the Wizard of Wurst's tower.

"Are you sure you want to go in there alone?" Lucas asked her.

"Of course," Princess Pulverizer replied.

"Besides, she's not *completely* alone," Dribble told Lucas. "You and I are going to be in spitting distance of that tower."

Princess Pulverizer wiggled
a rye seed loose from between
her teeth and spit it into the air.
The seed whirled.
It twirled.
It did a loop-the-
loop. And landed
right at the tower's
front door.
"Yup," she agreed.
"Spitting distance."

Princess Pulverizer reached into her sack and pulled out a shimmering ruby ring.

"You hold on to this for me," she told Lucas. "It's the ring the Queen of Shmergermeister gave me as a reward for returning her jewels. It's got magic powers."

"I remember," Lucas said. "Whoever wears it will walk with complete silence. No one will hear him coming."

"Exactly," Princess Pulverizer agreed. "That will give you the element of surprise in an emergency."

"E-e-emergency?" Lucas stammered nervously.

"I'll try not to give you any reason to use the ring," Princess Pulverizer assured him.

Lucas didn't look very comforted.

"I better get going," Princess Pulverizer said. "The sooner I get in there, the sooner I can rescue Lester the Jester."

Knock. Knock. Knock.

Princess Pulverizer bit her lip nervously as she knocked on the wizard's front door. She wondered if grown-up knights ever got scared. They didn't seem to. But who knew?

Maybe they just *pretended* to not be scared.

Knock. Knock. Knock.

Princess Pulverizer knocked even harder this time. She wanted to sound brave.

Finally, she heard footsteps coming from inside. The door opened. And there he was: the Wizard of Wurst.

Wow. The wizard didn't seem scary at all.

He was short and round, and his nose was squishy. He looked a little like a pig.

Princess Pulverizer breathed a sigh of relief.

There was nothing to be afraid of with this guy. He . . .

"WHAT DO YOU WANT?"

Gulp. Uh-oh. The wizard might not have looked scary, but he sure *sounded* scary.

"I . . . um . . . I want to be a wizard," Princess Pulverizer stammered nervously. "And I need you to teach me."

The wizard gave her an odd look. "*You* want to be a wizard?" he bellowed.

"Y-yes," Princess Pulverizer replied.

"But you're just a kid," the Wizard of Wurst said. "I don't want to be a babysitter."

That made the princess angry. She was no baby. And she didn't need to be sat. She was perfectly capable of taking care of herself, thank you very much.

But Princess Pulverizer didn't say that. She didn't want to make the Wizard of Wurst angry.

"I was told you are the wisest wizard in the world," she said instead.

"That's true," the Wizard of Wurst boasted.

"I want to learn from the best," Princess Pulverizer continued.

The wizard gave her a look. "I can't help feeling you're full of baloney," he said.

Actually, the princess was full of gouda from the grilled cheese sandwich she'd eaten that morning. But she didn't say that, either.

Instead, she replied, "I really want to learn to be a wizard. I'll do anything you ask. Mop your floors, feed the princes you've turned into frogs, stir your eye-of-newt stew—"

"I don't make eye-of-newt stew," the Wizard of Wurst interrupted her angrily. "That's for amateurs. I use eye of gecko. The spells last longer that way."

"You see, you've taught me something new already," Princess Pulverizer said. "You're not just a wise wizard, you're a *great* teacher."

"Yes, I am." The Wizard of Wurst puffed his chest proudly. "I suppose we can give it a try."

Princess Pulverizer grinned as she followed the Wizard of Wurst into his tower. Getting inside hadn't been difficult at all.

In fact, it had been kind of easy.

Still, as she walked through the dimly lit halls, making sure not to step on any of the mice that scurried angrily at her feet, Princess Pulverizer couldn't help feeling that the hard part was yet to come.

CHAPTER 5

"*Worms?*" Princess Pulverizer asked the wizard with surprise. "You turned a whole army of soldiers into *worms?*"

It was the middle of the afternoon, and for hours now the wizard had been bragging about the amazing things he'd done with his magic.

"Those soldiers came to steal from me," the Wizard of Wurst declared. "So I turned them into worms. Worms *can't* steal. They don't have any hands."

Princess Pulverizer stared nervously at the jar of worms. If she wasn't careful, she might wind up in there with them. The thought of it made her hands shake.

CRASH!

The jar of worms slipped from Princess Pulverizer's fingers and broke into pieces on the floor.

"Look what you've done!"

the Wizard of Wurst bellowed angrily. "You've freed my prisoners!"

Princess Pulverizer frowned as she looked at the worms that were now crawling around on the floor. Those were definitely *not* the prisoners she'd come here to free.

The wizard handed her an empty jar. "Catch those worms and put them in here. You better get every single one—if you know what's good for you."

Gulp. Princess Pulverizer dropped nervously to her knees and started picking up worms and dropping them into the jar. It wasn't easy. The worms were really slimy.

And to make matters worse, some of them were crawling over the broken glass. The sharp slivers cut them clean in half.

Strangely, the sliced worms didn't die. They kept on creeping and crawling.

Except now, where there had been only one worm, there were two.

And where there had been only two worms, there were four.

And where there had been only four

worms, there were eight.

Soon, there were *hundreds* of worms. They were everywhere.

Crawling into the corners.

Winding their way up the walls.

Wiggling onto the windowsills.

The Wizard of Wurst let out an evil laugh. "I'll meet you in my study when you've caught them all," he told Princess Pulverizer. *"If you ever do."*

By the time Princess Pulverizer had captured the very last worm, she was very tired. And hungry. And cranky.

"I've gotten them all," Princess Pulverizer told the Wizard of Wurst as she entered his study after hours of worm gathering.

"Took you long enough," he replied gruffly.

"There were a lot of worms," Princess Pulverizer explained. "And they kept slipping out of my hands."

"No excuses," the wizard huffed. He pointed to an extra magic wand on his desk. "Grab that. Let's do some magic!"

"Now?" the princess asked. "Can't I eat something first?"

"I've made you a liverwurst sandwich," the wizard said. "You can eat it later."

Princess Pulverizer glanced at the tiny sandwich on the wizard's desk. It was two pieces of white bread with a single slice of pale pink lunch meat slapped in between.

Some dinner that was.

What the princess wouldn't give for one of Dribble's grilled cheese sandwiches right around now.

Still, since the small black cat perched on the windowsill was also eyeing the sandwich, Princess Pulverizer figured she'd better get busy learning her magic spells if she was ever going to get to eat.

"I'm ready," she told the wizard.

"Let's start with something easy," the wizard said. "A growing spell."

"A what?" Princess Pulverizer asked.

"A growing spell." The wizard sounded annoyed to have to repeat himself. "Point the wand at something and come up with a rhyme to make it bigger."

Princess Pulverizer nodded. That didn't sound too tough. She just had to find something small that should be big.

Rumble. Grumble. Just then, the princess's empty stomach began to churn. Which gave her an idea.

Princess Pulverizer pointed her wand toward the liverwurst sandwich, and said, "I like things big. And I'm in charge. This object, once small, I will enlarge."

Poof! There was a flash of orange smoke. When it cleared, the princess came eye to eye with the largest mouse she had ever seen!

"MEEEEEOOOOOWWWWW!"
The cat took one look at the giant mouse
and raced out of the room.

"I'm sorry," Princess Pulverizer
apologized. "I was aiming for the
sandwich."

"You have lousy aim," the Wizard of
Wurst scolded her.

Princess Pulverizer didn't argue. How
could she? There was a giant mouse
standing right there in front of her.

The wizard pointed his wand at the
mouse and rhymed, "You're too tall, and
that's not right. Now be small and out of
sight."

Poof! There was a flash of yellow smoke.
When it cleared, the mouse was small
again.

The tiny creature stood there for a

moment, shocked. Then it scurried away into a hole in the wall—completely out of sight.

"You're good," Princess Pulverizer complimented the wizard.

"I'm *great*," the wizard countered. He plopped down on his couch and rested his feet on a nearby coffee table. The table shifted under the weight of his legs.

"I hate the way this wobbles," the wizard groaned. "That's your next task—fix the broken feet under this table."

Princess Pulverizer had watched her father's knights fix the Skround Table many times. A few taps with a hammer and the wizard's table should be good as new.

"Where do you keep the toolbox?" Princess Pulverizer asked.

The wizard rolled his eyes. "Use magic," he told her. "And try to aim the wand more carefully this time."

Princess Pulverizer was getting annoyed. What did the wizard expect from her? She bet he hadn't gotten everything right when he was first starting out.

Still, she carefully aimed her wand toward the bottom of the table and tried a spell. "The legs of this table move this way and that. When my wand gives a tap, its feet will stay flat."

Poof! There was a flash of purple smoke. When it cleared, the table's feet were flat to the floor. They had no arch at all.

That was the good news.

The bad news was that the feet now had *toes*. And those toes were tapping!

The next thing the princess knew, the

table started tap-dancing around the room.

The table danced its way through the door and into the hall.

It was heading toward the stairs when the Wizard of Wurst shouted, "Don't just stand there. Stop that crazy thing!"

Princess Pulverizer leaped on top of the dancing table.

The table reared forward, trying to throw her off.

The table shifted to the right.

It tilted to the left.

It turned in a circle.

But Princess Pulverizer couldn't be thrown.

The wizard stood angrily and pointed his wand. "Table, be again as you should," he chanted. "With a marble top and feet of wood."

Poof! There was a puff of hot pink smoke. When it cleared, the table had stopped tapping its toes. It didn't even *have* any toes. It just had wooden feet.

Wobbly wooden feet.

"Do you want me to try to fix it again?" Princess Pulverizer asked as she climbed off the table.

The Wizard of Wurst shook his head. "You've caused enough trouble for one day. I'm going to bed. You should, too. We have a lot of work to do in the morning."

"Okay," Princess Pulverizer agreed. "Where should I sleep?"

"Choose any room you want, except for the one at the end of the hallway. That's off-limits," the wizard warned her. "Good night."

As the Wizard of Wurst left his study and entered his bedroom, Princess Pulverizer smiled to herself. He had just given away a big secret.

There was only one reason a room might be off-limits. The wizard had to be hiding something really special in there.

Or some*one* really special.

Someone like Lester the Jester.

CHAPTER 6

CReak CReak

Princess Pulverizer really regretted leaving her ruby ring with Lucas. The floors in the tower were old and rickety. She couldn't take a single step without making noise.

Creak. Creak.

She tried to walk a little more quietly so she didn't wake the wizard. But Princess Pulverizer wasn't exactly light on her feet.

Finally, the princess reached the door at the end of the hallway. She reached out and turned the knob. But the door was locked. And there was no key in sight.

Now I'm really in a pickle, Princess Pulverizer thought to herself.

Grumble. Rumble.

At the mere thought of the word *pickle*, the princess's stomach started to groan.

She should have eaten that pathetic

liverwurst sandwich before she set off to rescue Lester the Jester. But that would have taken time. And frankly, the princess wanted to get out of this creepy tower as quickly as she could.

The sooner she freed Lester, the sooner she could get back to Lucas and Dribble— and to one of Dribble's delicious grilled cheese sandwiches. Maybe he would make her a cheddar cheese on rye. The princess really loved rye bread—seeds and all.

If only she could pick that lock.

Pick . . .

That's it! Princess Pulverizer thought. She reached into her knapsack and pulled out one of the small slivers of wood she used to pick rye seeds out of her teeth.

She slipped the slim toothpick into the keyhole.

She jiggled it to the right.

She joggled it to the left.

And then . . .

Click.

The lock popped open!

The princess smiled proudly as she slipped her toothpick back into her sack and turned the knob to the forbidden room.

The legendary knight Sir Loin hadn't been able to unlock the door to Lester the Jester's prison.

Neither had a whole army.

But she had been able to do it. And it hadn't taken her more than three seconds to figure out how.

Quickly, the princess turned the knob and burst through the door. "Lester the Jester, you are free! I, Princess Pulverizer, have rescued . . . *oh*!"

The princess stopped talking as soon as she entered the room.

That was when she realized that she hadn't freed Lester at all.

He was trapped in a giant cage that was kept behind the locked door.

That meant there were two locks.

One on the door.

And one on the cage.

"You were saying?" Lester the Jester replied, glaring at her from behind the cage's thick metal bars.

At least Princess Pulverizer *assumed* the man in the cage was Lester. They hadn't been properly introduced. But judging by the funny hat on his head, and the bells on the tips of his shoes, she figured that was who he had to be.

"Um . . . I was saying that I, Princess Pulverizer, have *arrived to rescue* you," the princess corrected herself.

Lester looked her up and down. "*Salami* get this straight—I'm going to be rescued by a kid?" he asked her with a laugh. "Impossible."

Princess Pulverizer frowned angrily. "I'm not just any kid," she insisted. "I'm Princess Pulverizer. I'm strong. And really smart. I figured out a way to get in here even though the door was locked, didn't I?"

Lester rolled his eyes. "You're not the first one to get into this room," he told her. "The great Sir Loin was here. A whole army of Salamistonia's finest soldiers made it past that door. But none of them were able to get me out of this cage."

"I've met that army," Princess Pulverizer told him. "They seemed pretty wormy to me."

Lester sighed. "Go back to your castle, Princess. You do know how to get home, don't you? Follow the foot-*prince*."

Princess Pulverizer groaned. "That's an awful joke," she told him.

"What do you expect?" Lester replied. "Do you have any idea how hard it is to be funny when you're locked up in a cage?"

Princess Pulverizer looked around the room. There had to be some way to free Lester.

Just then, the princess spied a giant key. It was hanging from a hook on the wall—just out of Lester's reach.

"The wizard put the key right where you can see it, but you can't get to it," Princess Pulverizer said. "That's mean."

"The wizard's a pretty mean guy," Lester replied. "In case you hadn't noticed."

Princess Pulverizer *had* noticed. Turning soldiers into worms definitely wasn't nice. There was no telling what the wizard would turn *her* into if he woke up and found her in here talking to Lester the Jester.

Quickly, Princess Pulverizer yanked the heavy key from its hook. She jammed it into the lock and turned it.

But the lock didn't open.

"Um . . . aren't you forgetting something?" Lester pointed out.

"What?" Princess Pulverizer asked as she tried over and over to turn the key.

"There's a spell on that lock," Lester said. "You can't open it unless you are selfless and pure of heart. And something tells me you're not either of those."

Oops. Princess Pulverizer had forgotten all about that.

The princess knew she was brave and smart. But that didn't make her selfless.

In fact, some people might say she was a little sel*fish*.

Not to mention spoiled.

And stubborn.

Those things probably kept a girl from being pure of heart.

"Face it, Princess, you're not cut out for the rescuing business," Lester told her. Now Princess Pulverizer was getting really angry. Lester the Jester was one ungrateful jerk. Here she was risking her life to save him, and he was being awful.

"I have half a mind to just leave you here," Princess Pulverizer told him angrily.

"Half a mind sounds about right," Lester agreed. "But that's okay. Princesses are rich. You can hire someone to do your thinking for you."

"I'm not the one who got myself caught and put in a cage," Princess Pulverizer told him.

"Not *yet*," Lester reminded her.

Suddenly, the princess heard noises coming from the hallway. "What's that?" she asked Lester nervously.

"Sounds like the Wizard of Wurst is sleepwalking again. He does that sometimes." Lester glanced at the expression on Princess Pulverizer's face. "Oh, don't look so scared. You're okay— as long as he doesn't wake up and find you here."

Princess Pulverizer gulped. "I have

to go now," she told Lester.

"Yeah, I figured a kid like you was sure to chicken out," Lester replied. "And speaking of chickens—do you know what you call a crazy chicken?"

"No," Princess Pulverizer replied. "What?"

"A cuckoo cluck," Lester told her. He began laughing hysterically.

Princess Pulverizer frowned. That joke was horrible.

She had to free Lester, and soon. He was already forgetting how to be funny. And if he couldn't be funny anymore, it wouldn't matter whether she got him back to Salamistonia or not. Because the whole point was to make the people laugh again. And no chicken joke was going to do that.

"Don't worry, I'm not a chicken,"

Princess Pulverizer promised Lester as she hurried for the door. "I'll be back—just as soon as I figure out a way to open that lock!"

"*If* you figure out a way," Lester called after her. "And from where I'm sitting, that's a very big *if*."

CHAPTER 7

"Turning princes into toads is easy. Turning them into frogs is *not*."

It was early the next afternoon, and the wizard was teaching Princess Pulverizer about spells that transformed one thing into another.

"The problem is, you have to get the prince near water to turn him into a frog," the Wizard of Wurst continued. "These days, princes don't like to go *near* water.

They're all too afraid of messing up their hair."

That made Princess Pulverizer smile. She knew how vain princes could be. She'd caught more than a few fixing their hair in her father's mirrored ballroom.

"Did I tell you about the footman I hired to clean my silver and dust my furniture?" the wizard continued.

That surprised Princess Pulverizer. She hadn't seen *any* servants in the tower. As far as she knew, it was just the wizard and her—and Lester the Jester.

"Do you still have a footman?" she asked the wizard curiously.

"No," the Wizard of Wurst replied. "Now I have a foot*stool*. That's what I turned the footman into when I caught him stealing my silverware."

A foot*stool*? Quickly, Princess Pulverizer took her feet off the stool in front of her. As she put her feet on the ground, she swore she heard a tiny voice say, "Thanks."

The wizard walked across the room and suddenly flung open the doors that led to the balcony.

Princess Pulverizer took a deep breath. It was the first fresh air she'd felt on her face since she'd entered the wizard's tower. She wished she were out there in the woods with Dribble and Lucas, enjoying the great outdoors, instead of being stuck here with the wizard.

"Come here," the Wizard of Wurst commanded. "I want you to meet the latest victim of my magic."

The princess walked out onto the balcony and looked around.

Coo. Coo. Suddenly, she heard a pigeon.

Sure enough, in the corner of the balcony there was a small pigeon coop. Inside the coop was one lonely white pigeon with just a splash of gray on his wing feathers.

"Meet Jacob," the wizard introduced him. "He said he wanted to be my apprentice and learn magic—just like you. But I soon learned that wasn't why he was here at all."

Now the wizard had Princess Pulverizer's attention.

"Jacob was a spy for the Wild Witch of Sandwich," the Wizard of Wurst continued. "She sent him here to learn my magic tricks so she could use them against me. I don't take kindly to apprentices helping my enemies."

Gulp. Princess Pulverizer wasn't sure if that was a warning—or if the wizard was actually on to her. Either way, it was making her very nervous.

Maybe it was best if she left without trying to rescue Lester the Jester.

Why should she risk spending her life covered in feathers for a guy who didn't like her anyway?

Lester was mean.

And nasty.

And not particularly funny.

Was he really worth rescuing?

Unfortunately, the answer was *yes*. It was a knight's job to save people who were in trouble—whether she liked them or not.

Princess Pulverizer was going to have to find someone who was pure of heart and have him—or her—open Lester's cell.

Because she wasn't going to be able to do it. If the princess was being honest, she was only interested in saving Lester so she could get closer to her goal of getting into Knight School.

Which was not exactly the way somebody selfless and pure of heart would act.

Grrr. This was so frustrating. The princess had been in the tower two days already and she was no closer to freeing Lester.

To make matters worse, there was nothing to eat in this place but liverwurst.

Liverwurst and eggs for breakfast.

Liverwurst on white bread for lunch.

A liverwurst cookie for a snack.

That cookie had been *especially* disgusting. Liverwurst doesn't taste so great when it's dunked in milk. What Princess Pulverizer wouldn't give for one of Dribble's sandwiches right now.

Princess Pulverizer didn't just miss Dribble's cooking. She missed everything about the big guy. The way he smiled when she made a joke, and how he burped when he'd had too much to eat.

The princess missed Lucas, too. Sure, he was afraid of his own shadow—*literally*. She had actually seen him try to run away from it! But Lucas was a wonderful friend. He saw the good in everyone. His best friend was a dragon that everyone else feared.

Even Princess Pulverizer had doubted Dribble when they first met. She had been pretty mean to him. But Lucas didn't even know *how* to be mean. He was . . .

Selfless and pure of heart! That was it. Lucas was going to have to be the one to free Lester the Jester!

It was the perfect plan.

Except for one little detail.

Well, a *big* detail, actually.

Lucas wasn't in the tower. He was out in the woods with Dribble. And the princess had no way of getting a message to him.

She couldn't just ask to go for a walk in the woods. The wizard was watching her way too closely. And he might not let her back in.

Coo. Coo. Jacob flapped his wings and

moved sadly to the other side of the coop.

"Stop that!" the Wizard of Wurst shouted. "I can't teach if you're making noise."

Coo. Coo, the pigeon repeated.

"Sometimes I just want to let that pigeon loose in the forest," the wizard groaned angrily to Princess Pulverizer. "But with my luck, he'd fly right back here."

Princess Pulverizer's eyes opened wide. Her heart thumped excitedly. The Wizard of Wurst didn't know it, but he'd just given her a great idea.

Now she knew how to get a message to Dribble and Lucas!

As the Wizard of Wurst went back into his office, Princess Pulverizer snuck a few bits of bread from her sandwich into Jacob's cage.

The pigeon pecked hungrily at the scraps and looked up at the princess gratefully.

Princess Pulverizer smiled and snuck him a few more pieces of bread. It was important that she be on the pigeon's good side.

After all, Jacob was going to have to be the one to save the day!

That night, after the Wizard of Wurst went to bed, Princess Pulverizer snuck out of the small room near the stairs that she had chosen as her bedroom. She tiptoed quietly onto the balcony outside the wizard's office. Then she walked over to the pigeon coop and knelt down so Jacob could hear her clearly.

"I'm going to set you free," she whispered to the pigeon.

Jacob looked up at her curiously and cooed.

"Shhhh . . . ," the princess warned nervously. The last thing she needed was for Jacob to wake the Wizard of Wurst.

"I need you to fly this note to my friends in the woods," Princess Pulverizer explained as she held up a small slip of paper. "After that, you can try to find your way home. Maybe the Wild Witch of Sandwich knows how to turn you back into a person."

Jacob cooed and nodded his head up and down.

He understood!

Or at least Princess Pulverizer *hoped* he understood. It was hard to tell. Pigeons were always cooing and nodding their heads up and down.

Princess Pulverizer opened the pigeon coop and carried Jacob over to the edge of the balcony. She tucked her note into his beak, held him up, and . . .

Uh-oh.

There was a slight problem with Princess Pulverizer's plan.

Make that a *huge* problem.

She didn't know where to point the pigeon.

Princess Pulverizer looked out over the vast forest below. Dribble and Lucas could be hiding anywhere out there.

Just then, Princess Pulverizer saw billowy smoke coming from a cluster

‹84›

of giant evergreen trees that were very close by.

Dribble made a lot of smoke when he cooked grilled cheese.

That had to be them—it just *had* to be.

"Okay, Jacob," Princess Pulverizer said as she set the pigeon free. "Fly to where you see the smoke. Give my friends the message."

Princess Pulverizer crossed her fingers for luck as Jacob took off into the night sky. She needed the pigeon to get that message to Dribble and Lucas.

Lester the Jester's freedom—and the fate of Salamistonia—depended on it.

CHAPTER 8

Princess Pulverizer looked to the left.

She looked to the right.

She twiddled her thumbs.

And wiggled her toes.

The waiting was making her crazy.

It was morning already, and Lucas and Dribble had still not arrived.

Scary thoughts were flying through the princess's brain.

What if Jacob hadn't gotten her message to them?

What if Jacob *had* gotten her message to them but they'd decided not to come?

What if they had gotten lost on their way to the tower?

And then there was the scariest thought of all: What was going to happen to her when the Wizard of Wurst discovered Jacob was gone? Without Dribble and Lucas to help her, it would be just her against the wizard.

Princess Pulverizer didn't like those odds one bit.

"ARE YOU LISTENING TO ME?"

the Wizard of Wurst bellowed at her.

That snapped Princess Pulverizer back to attention. "Yes. I'm listening."

"Good," the wizard said. "Now, because we are outside, you have to be very careful with the way you aim the wand. There are no walls to contain your magic."

Princess Pulverizer nodded.

"You see that snake?" the wizard asked, pointing to a green-and-yellow garden snake resting beneath a big apple tree. "Turn it into a cow. We need fresh milk."

Princess Pulverizer walked over to the snake and pointed her wand. "Sorry about this," she whispered to him. Then, in a loud, firm voice, she chanted, "We can't drink snake poison if we want to live. So turn this snake to a bovine with fresh milk to give."

There was a flash of green smoke. When it cleared, the princess saw a long, thin vine with green and yellow leaves slithering up the side of the tower.

"What have you done *now*?" the Wizard of Wurst asked angrily.

"I just tried to turn the snake into a cow," the princess told him.

"But you didn't *say* cow," the wizard pointed out. "You said bo*vine*."

"Which is another word for cow," Princess Pulverizer insisted. "I was being creative."

"Did I say you could be creative?" the Wizard of Wurst shouted. "You are the worst wizard's apprentice ever!"

A slow grin began to form on Princess Pulverizer's lips.

"What are you smiling about?" the wizard demanded angrily.

"Um . . . nothing," Princess Pulverizer lied.

Actually, the princess had good reason to smile. She had just spotted Lucas and Dribble sneaking out from the woods.

Luckily, the wizard hadn't heard anyone sneaking up behind him.

The Queen of Shmergermeister's ruby ring was sitting on the tip of Dribble's tail. So the dragon was walking in complete silence. And since Lucas was riding on Dribble's back, *his* feet weren't making any sounds, either.

Princess Pulverizer was very impressed. Putting the ring on Dribble's tail was a stroke of genius. The wizard had no idea . . .

"AAAAACHOOOOOO!"

Suddenly, Dribble let out one of his giant dragon-sized sneezes.

The sneeze was so loud and powerful, it knocked the wizard to the ground with a *thud*. His magic wand flew out of his hand.

Princess Pulverizer frowned. *So much for the element of surprise.*

"Sorry," Dribble apologized. He wiped a dragon-sized booger from his nostril. "I have allergies."

Before the wizard had a chance to get back on his feet, Princess Pulverizer leaped into action, ripping the vine from the wall and wrapping it tightly around the wizard's body, making sure his legs were bound together and his hands were tied tightly to his sides. Now, even if the wizard could somehow reach his magic wand, he wouldn't be able to aim it.

"You traitor!" the Wizard of Wurst cried out.

Princess Pulverizer was sick and tired of hearing the wizard's ranting and raving. She grabbed an apple and shoved it into his mouth. Now he couldn't speak, either.

Lucas and Dribble stared at her in amazement.

"I've never seen anyone move so fast before," Lucas said.

Princess Pulverizer smiled proudly. But this was no time for compliments. It probably wouldn't take long for the wizard to untangle himself from the vines. So unless they wanted to become worms, pigeons, footstools, or something much, *much* worse, she knew they'd better get moving.

"Come on, you guys," Princess Pulverizer ordered as she raced toward the tower. "We've got a jester to free!"

CHapteR 9

"Why me?" Lucas asked a few minutes later. He was facing a corner of the room, several steps away from Lester's cage, shaking with fright.

"Because you're the only one who can do it," Princess Pulverizer insisted.

"But I don't want to be the one who breaks the Wizard of Wurst's magic spell," Lucas insisted. "If I do, I'll be the one he's maddest at."

"You *have* to open the lock, Lucas," Princess Pulverizer insisted. "I can't do it, because I'm not selfless or pure of heart."

"What about Dribble?" Lucas asked her.

"I don't have thumbs," Dribble explained. "You can't turn a key without thumbs."

Lucas frowned. "I never thought of that."

"It's not always easy being a dragon," Dribble admitted.

"Hey, big guy," Lester called to Dribble. "You know what time it is when a dragon sits on your fence?"

"What time?" Dribble asked him.

"Time to get a new fence." Lester started laughing.

"That's not funny," Dribble replied.

"Everybody's a critic," the jester muttered under his breath.

"This is no time for joking around, Lester," Princess Pulverizer told him.

"We've got to get you out of here. Please, Lucas. You just have to—"

But before Princess Pulverizer could finish her sentence, she heard the wizard's angry voice coming from the hallway.

"MOVE IT!" he shouted.

Uh-oh! The wizard had obviously spit

out the apple the princess had shoved in his mouth. Now he was free to bark orders.

But how had he managed to get up the stairs with his arms and legs tied up?

The princess ran to the doorway—just in time to see a whole army of worms slithering right toward her.

The worms were carrying the Wizard of Wurst down the hall on their backs!

"Faster, you army of spineless, slimy slitherers!" the Wizard of Wurst commanded. "Or I will turn you into something a lot worse than worms!"

The worms slithered faster. They were obviously taking the wizard's threats very seriously.

Princess Pulverizer gulped. "Come on, Lucas," she said, trying to remain calm. "You have to free Lester right now. *The Wizard of Wurst is on his way!*"

"Bet you can't say that five times fast," Lester joked.

Princess Pulverizer ignored him. "Please, Lucas," she urged.

But by now the wizard had arrived. The very sight of him made Lucas shake.

"Don't worry about the wizard," Princess Pulverizer said. "He can't do anything without his magic wand."

"Look behind me," the Wizard of Wurst told her.

Uh-oh. Out in the hallway, the princess spotted a long, skinny worm. He was slithering along with the wizard's magic wand on his back.

Lucas began to cry.

"There's nothing to worry about," Princess Pulverizer soothed. "The wizard's arms are tied to his sides. He can't aim his wand. He can't even reach it."

The wizard shot Princess Pulverizer an evil grin. "That's what you think," he replied. Then he barked out a new order. "Mouse! Start chewing! Or else!"

Immediately, a tiny frightened mouse scurried to the wizard's side and began chomping away at the vine that was wrapped around his body.

Within seconds, the Wizard of Wurst was free. He leaped to his feet and grabbed his wand.

"FROZEN WITH FEAR, ARE YOU?" the wizard asked Lucas. "I can make sure you stay that way."

"Wh-wh-what does that mean?" Lucas stammered.

The wizard pointed his wand straight at Lucas. "You've come to release Lester. But your mission is lost. With a wave of my wand, you'll be frozen in fro—"

"No, you don't!" Princess Pulverizer shouted out. Before the wizard could finish the word *frost*, she leaped in front of Lucas—without a single thought for her own safety.

"Aachoo!" Dribble sneezed wildly. His tail swung around, and *bam*—knocked the magic wand right out of the wizard's hand!

Princess Pulverizer reached out and caught the wand in midair.

"Frost!" the wizard said, finishing his spell.

"I'm rubber, you're glue!" Princess Pulverizer called back to him, waving the wand at the wizard. "Your words bounce off me and stick to you."

It was a lousy spell, and the princess knew it.

There was a good chance that any minute now she'd be frozen solid.

Suddenly, there was a flash of ice-blue smoke. And when it cleared . . .

The Wizard of Wurst was standing there. *Frozen*. He looked like an ice statue.

But Princess Pulverizer wasn't even a bit chilly.

Princess Pulverizer stared at the Wizard of Wurst with surprise.

That spell *couldn't* have worked.

It *shouldn't* have worked.

Except it had.

"You did it!" Dribble cheered.

"Okay, Lucas, you're safe now," Princess Pulverizer assured her pal. "Open the lock."

Lucas moved closer to Lester's cage. But his hand was shaking so hard, he could not fit the key into the lock. "I—I—I can't do it," he stammered helplessly. "I can't stop shaking. It takes me a while to calm down."

Unfortunately, they didn't have a while. Princess Pulverizer slumped. "I'm out of ideas," she admitted. "I'm sorry, Lester."

"This isn't over," Dribble insisted.

Princess Pulverizer gave him a sad, defeated look. "It is, Dribble," she said. "Lucas can't do this. He's too afraid."

"But *you're* not," Dribble reminded her. "You're never afraid."

That wasn't exactly true. Princess Pulverizer was afraid sometimes.

Not that it mattered. "Fear isn't the problem," she explained. "I can't open the lock because I'm not selfless or pure of heart."

Dribble shook his head. "I just saw you jump in front of Lucas when you thought the wizard might hurt him. If you ask me, that was pretty selfless. And pure of heart."

Hmmm . . . That's true.

"It's worth a try," Princess Pulverizer agreed finally. She took the key from Lucas and inserted it into the lock. Then, ever so slowly, she gave it a turn.

CLICK.

The lock popped open!

"Woohoo!" Lester pushed open the door of his cage. "I'm out of here!"

"Right behind you!" Princess Pulverizer started toward the door, stopping only to admire the Wizard of Wurst's wand in her hand. It was proof of the good deed she had just accomplished. She knew her father would be impressed.

"Come on, Lucas," Dribble said. "It's time to go."

But Lucas wouldn't move. He just stood there. Petrified. Again.

"What are you afraid of now?" Dribble asked him. "The wizard can't hurt us. He's frozen solid."

Lucas pointed at the army of worms. "I hate creepy-crawly things."

"Don't be afraid of them," Princess Pulverizer said. "They were once an army, mighty and strong. But to fear them now is just plain wrong."

Poof! Suddenly, there was a flash of purple smoke. And when it cleared . . .

Princess Pulverizer was standing face-to-face with an army of soldiers.

Tall, strong soldiers.

Soldiers who had *swords*.

"What did you just do?" Dribble asked
Princess Pulverizer nervously.

"I must have been aiming the wand at
the worms when I said they were an army,

mighty and strong," Princess Pulverizer answered. "I didn't mean it to be a spell."

"You gotta be more careful where you point that thing," Lucas told her.

As if being surrounded by armed soldiers wasn't bad enough, the sun was now high in the sky. The tower was getting warm. Before long, the wizard would defrost. And when he did, he was sure to be angry.

The princess and her friends had to get out of the tower.

Unfortunately, the soldiers had them surrounded.

"Um . . . what's that guy doing?" Dribble pointed to a soldier who had just pulled his sword from its sheath.

Lucas started to cry. Again. "We're done for!"

Princess Pulverizer didn't blame Lucas for being afraid. This time, it really did seem like they were in trouble.

She stared up at the soldier's long, sharp sword, and studied his angry, mean . . .

Hey! Wait a minute.

The soldier didn't look mean.

Or angry.

Or scary.

And he wasn't aiming his sword at her, either. He was raising it victoriously straight up in the air.

And he was *smiling*.

In fact, *all* the soldiers were smiling.

"Hail, hail Princess Pulverizer!" another soldier cried out, raising his sword in victory, too. "She's freed us."

Soon, all the soldiers were cheering. "Three cheers for Princess Pulverizer!"

"*Whoa!*" Princess Pulverizer gasped as one of the soldiers lifted her in the air.

Whoops. The magic wand slipped from the princess's hand as she struggled to hold on to the soldier's shoulders.

"Somebody grab that wand!" the princess shouted.

But the soldiers didn't hear her. They were cheering too loudly. "Hip, hip, hooray for Princess Pulverizer!"

Crack.

Crunch.

Snap.

As they marched out of the tower, the soldiers stomped on the wizard's magic wand, breaking it into pieces.

So much for proof of the princess's good deed.

"What a waste of time," she grumbled as

the army carried her out of the tower and onto the road that led to Salamistonia.

"It wasn't a waste of time," Dribble disagreed, as he marched alongside her with Lucas on his back. "You turned the worms back into soldiers."

"And you freed Lester the Jester," Lucas added.

From her perch high up on the soldier's shoulders, Princess Pulverizer could see Lester the Jester happily leaping and spinning his way down the road.

"I really relish the idea of finally eating a delicious salami on rye," Lester shouted gleefully. "Get it? *Relish?*"

"That's the wurst joke I ever heard," Dribble groaned. "Besides, I'd rather have a grilled cheese sandwich."

"Do you know what you call the watery

cheese you find around a castle?" Princess Pulverizer asked Dribble.

"No," the dragon replied. "What?"

"*Moat*-zarella cheese!" Princess Pulverizer laughed at her own joke.

Dribble and Lucas started laughing, too. So did a few of the soldiers.

But Lester wasn't laughing. "Stop being such a *ham*," he called back to her. "*I'm* the jester here, remember?"

CHAPTER 10

"So I told the vegetarian, you're making a big mis-*steak*!" Lester the Jester said, finishing a joke he'd been telling in the King of Salamistonia's banquet hall that evening.

Everyone in the room started laughing.

Well, everyone except Dribble, Lucas, and Princess Pulverizer, anyway.

"I don't get it," Dribble whispered.

"Me either," Lucas admitted.

"But everyone else is laughing. Maybe we're missing something."

"It doesn't matter," Princess Pulverizer told her friends. "The point is Lester's back, and the people of Salamistonia are happy again."

Dribble took a lick of his dessert and made a face. "Why would anyone think a salami-flavored ice cream sundae was a good idea? This stuff is gross."

"I know," Lucas agreed. "What's this gooey yellow gunk dripping all over the ice cream?"

"Mustard sauce," Princess Pulverizer told him.

"I can't eat this stuff," Dribble groaned.

"Shhh . . . ," Princess Pulverizer whispered. "The king is about to speak."

All eyes turned to the head of the table as the King of Salamistonia stood and raised his goblet.

"I'd like to thank the person responsible for bringing laughter back to Salamistonia," the king said.

Lester stood up tall. He puffed his chest proudly.

"To Princess Pulverizer!" the king continued.

"To Princess Pulverizer," the guests echoed, raising their drinks as well.

Lester slumped over and frowned. "Hey, what about me?" he muttered.

The King of Salamistonia smiled at Princess Pulverizer. "Thank you," he said.

"You're welcome," Princess Pulverizer replied. "But I didn't do it alone."

Once again, Lester stood tall and puffed his chest.

"Lucas and Dribble helped a great deal," the princess continued.

Lester groaned. "I don't get any respect," he said.

"We are a team," Princess Pulverizer said, smiling at Lucas and Dribble. "It takes the power of three to defeat evil people like the Wizard of Wurst."

"I salute all three of you," the king replied. "And as a token of my gratitude, I am presenting you with this sword."

Princess Pulverizer smiled as she took the sword from the King of Salamistonia. Now she had a token she could show her father.

"Thank you," she told the king. "I will treasure it."

"I hope you will also *use* it," the king said. "Because that sword has magical powers. It can reveal when someone is being untruthful."

Lucas looked at the sword. "How can a sword do that?" he wondered.

"All you have to do is point it directly at someone," the king explained. "If he is telling the truth, the sword will remain  still. But if he is lying, it will begin to quiver."

"That is sure to come in handy,"
Princess Pulverizer agreed. "Thank you."

"You're welcome," the king replied. "I
hope you all enjoyed your dinner tonight."

"It was delicious," Dribble told him.

Princess Pulverizer pointed the sword at
the dragon. Instantly, it began to quiver.

Dribble's cheeks turned purple—which
was what happened whenever the dragon
was embarrassed. "Um . . . I mean . . .
it . . ."

The king laughed. "Salami-flavored ice
cream isn't for everyone," he admitted.

Then he turned to Lester. "Isn't there
something you want to tell our guests?"
he asked the jester.

"Sure," Lester agreed. "Do you know
what the groceries said when the lettuce
brought a salami to the party?"

The king shook his head. "No kidding around, Lester. You need to thank them for freeing you."

"Oh, *that*," Lester said. "Thank you. I'm really glad to be home again. And that's no joke."

"You're welcome," Princess Pulverizer replied. She reached out and shook his hand.

"So, I guess this is goodbye, then," Lester said.

"Oh, we're not saying goodbye," Princess Pulverizer replied.

"We're not?" Dribble asked.

"You mean we're staying here?" Lucas wondered. He sounded very confused.

"No, we're leaving," the princess assured her friends. "But we're not saying goodbye. We're saying, 'Until we *meat* again!'"

THE QUEST
CONTINUES . . .

and now, here's a
sneak peek at the next

Princess PULVERIZER

Bad moooove!

"*Cheddar, swiss, and fresh ricotta.*
Grilled cheese on rye is a party start-a.
Gouda, brie, and a mild havarti.
Cheese is welcome at any party.
Oh yeah, yeah, yeah. Whoa, whoa, whoa."
Dribble the dragon was happily singing
his favorite song as his best friend, Lucas,
danced along. They were both in a really
good mood this sunny morning.

"I love that song," Lucas said as he kicked his legs and wiggled his hips. *Clink. Clank. Clunk.* His heavy suit of armor set the beat as he danced.

"Me too," Dribble agreed. "Who doesn't love a good cheese song?"

Princess Pulverizer, that's who.

The princess wasn't enjoying Dribble's song at all. She was sitting by the riverbank with her hands clapped over her ears. She had a really sour look on her face. Even more sour than a big hunk of tyrolean gray cheese.

But Dribble and Lucas weren't about to let a grumpy princess stop their fun. So Dribble kept singing. And Lucas kept dancing.

"Roquefort, taleggio, and a smelly blue. The stinkier the better, they say that's true."

"Will you cut that out?!" Princess Pulverizer shouted angrily.

Dribble stopped singing.

Lucas stopped dancing.

They both stared at her.

"Come on," Dribble said, trying to urge the princess out of her bad mood. "It's a gorgeous day. The birds are tweeting. The crickets are chirping. *Everyone's* singing."

"And you're *all* making me nuts," Princess Pulverizer replied.

"Why are you in such a lousy mood?" Lucas asked the princess.

"Because we're just sitting here, doing nothing," Princess Pulverizer told him.

"No we're not," Lucas said. "Dribble is singing. And I'm dancing."

"But you're not *supposed* to be singing and dancing," Princess Pulverizer told

Lucas. "We are supposed to be out there helping people. That's what a Quest of Kindness is all about."

"Oh, *that* again." Dribble groaned.

"Yes, *that* again," Princess Pulverizer told him. "We haven't helped anyone since we freed Lester the Jester from the clutches of the evil Wizard of Wurst."

"That's because we haven't come across anyone in trouble," Lucas said. "Which, if you think about it, is a good thing."

"No it's not," Princess Pulverizer insisted.

Dribble and Lucas stared at her.

"I didn't mean it like that," Princess Pulverizer explained. "I don't like seeing people in trouble. But I really do need to find someone to save. You guys understand that, don't you?"

Dribble and Lucas both nodded. They understood exactly what she meant.

Princess Pulverizer wasn't your average princess. She didn't want to dance the saltarello at royal balls, sip tea with her pinkie in the air at fancy lunches, or balance a heavy crown on top of her head as she welcomed princes into her castle.

That was because Princess Pulverizer didn't want to *be* a princess.

She wanted to be a *knight*. A full-fledged, horseback-riding, armor-wearing, damsel-in-distress-saving kind of knight.

And to do that, she would have to go to Knight School.

Her father, King Alexander, had actually said she could go—on one condition. She had to complete eight good deeds on a Quest of Kindness. Once she had done that, she could get her first set of armor and enter Knight School.

King Alexander had explained that knights were selfless people who spent their lives helping others. A Quest of Kindness would teach Princess Pulverizer to care about other people, the way all good knights did.

So now Princess Pulverizer was traveling the countryside trying to find folks who needed her help. She really, really, *really* wanted to take her place among King Alexander's Knights of the Skround Table.

But doing good deeds was hard work. Luckily for the princess, she had stumbled upon Dribble and Lucas. They were a great help to her, which might surprise a lot of people. After all, Lucas was such a fraidy-cat that the other boys had nicknamed him Lucas the Lily-Livered and laughed him out of Knight School. And Dribble had been banished from his lair because, unlike other dragons, he used his fire for making grilled cheese sandwiches rather than burning down villages.

But Dribble and Lucas were a lot smarter and tougher than they seemed. The princess and her pals had already used their combined talents to defeat two very tough enemies. Unfortunately, that still left six good deeds to go before Princess Pulverizer could return home with eight tokens in hand.

Princess Pulverizer was not exactly known for her patience.

"Someone who needs our help will come along eventually," Dribble assured her. "But for now, let's enjoy this beautiful day." He began singing again.

"*Cheddar.*"

Lucas twirled out onto a long, thick log that was sticking way out into the river.

"*Swiss.*"

Lucas whirled around in a circle.

"*And fresh ricotta . . .*"

SPLASH! Lucas twirled and whirled his way off the log and right into the river.

"HELP!" Lucas shouted as he struggled to keep his head above water. "HELP!"

"His armor is weighing him down," Dribble gasped. "He's going to drown!"

"I'll save him!" Princess Pulverizer kicked off her shoes and dived into the water.

She grinned happily as she swam to her friend's aid. Finally, the princess had a good deed to do. Lucas sure was a good pal to fall into the river just to help her out. Any second now she would . . .

Oh no!

Princess Pulverizer looked at Lucas and frowned.

While she had been swimming over to Lucas, Dribble had balanced himself on the long, thick log where Lucas had been dancing and simply *walked* over to where Lucas was bobbing up and down frantically. Now he was holding out his tail like a green safety line.

"Grab on, little buddy," Dribble called to Lucas. "I'll pull you out!"

Princess Pulverizer watched irritably as Lucas grasped the edge of Dribble's tail and held on as the dragon dragged him back to shore.

Princess Pulverizer swam back to the riverbank and climbed out of the water. "What did you do that for?" she demanded.

Dribble shrugged. "I couldn't let him drown. He's my best friend."

"I was swimming to him," the princess insisted. "*I* was supposed to save him."

"You swim too slowly. He would have gone under for good by the time you got there," Dribble told her. "My tail was faster."

It was hard to argue with that.

"Fine," Princess Pulverizer huffed angrily. "But now we have to get going. I need to find someone *else* to help before the sun goes down."

"Maybe we should wait on that," Lucas suggested.

"Why?" Princess Pulverizer asked impatiently.

"Because you and I stink of fish." Lucas reached into his helmet and pulled out a flipping-flopping trout. "Nobody wants to be saved by a smelly knight," he added as he threw the fish back into the water.

Hmmm. He had a point there.

But Princess Pulverizer didn't want to wait for the fishy stink to disappear. That could take a long time. There had to be some way to get rid of the smell.

Out of the corner of her eye, Princess Pulverizer spotted a patch of pretty pink flowers. *Yes! That's it!*

The princess reached down and yanked the pretty posies right out of the ground— roots and all. She shoved a few of them into her hair and a few more into Lucas's visor.

"Now we smell like flowers!" she told Lucas excitedly. "Problem solved."

Dribble wrinkled his snout. "Not exactly. Now you smell like fish *and* flowers."

"It's good enough," Princess Pulverizer insisted. "Come on. We—"

"BEE!" Lucas shouted, interrupting her and taking off. He tried to outrun a bumblebee that had been resting in one of the flowers Princess Pulverizer had shoved into his helmet. "GET AWAY FROM ME, BEE!"

Princess Pulverizer had never seen Lucas move that quickly. But she was glad he was moving. Now they could finally get on with their quest.

The faster they ran, the faster they could find someone in need of their help.

Of course, if Lucas was way ahead of her, he might stumble across someone to help before she did.

Princess Pulverizer could *not* let that happen.

"Wait for me!" she shouted to Lucas. "If anyone's gonna save someone, it's gonna be me."

"*Ahem*," Dribble said, giving her an angry look.

"Oh, right," Princess Pulverizer corrected herself. "I meant wait for Dribble *and* me! Good deeds are easier when you have the power of three!"

to be continued . . .

PRINCESS PULVERIZER

collect each adventure on your reading quest!

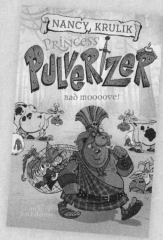

author & illustrator

Nancy Krulik

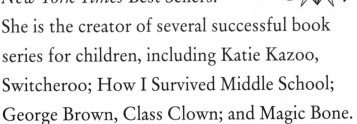

is the author of more than two hundred books for children and young adults, including three *New York Times* Best Sellers.

She is the creator of several successful book series for children, including Katie Kazoo, Switcheroo; How I Survived Middle School; George Brown, Class Clown; and Magic Bone.

Ben Balistreri

has been working for more than twenty years in the animation industry. He's won an Emmy Award for his character designs and has been nominated for nine Annie Awards, winning once. His art can be seen in *Tangled: The Series*, *How to Train Your Dragon*, and many more.